T0413432

I Know the Rules!

I LISTEN!

By Bray Jacobson

Gareth Stevens
PUBLISHING

Please visit our website, www.garethstevens.com. For a free color catalog of all our high-quality books, call toll free 1-800-542-2595 or fax 1-877-542-2596.

Library of Congress Cataloging-in-Publication Data

Names: Jacobson, Bray, author.
Title: I listen! / Bray Jacobson.
Description: Buffalo, New York : Gareth Stevens Publishing, [2024] | Series: I know the rules! | Includes index.
Identifiers: LCCN 2022051538 (print) | LCCN 2022051539 (ebook) | ISBN 9781538286623 (library binding) | ISBN 9781538286616 (paperback) | ISBN 9781538286630 (ebook)
Subjects: LCSH: Listening–Juvenile literature. | Social skills in children–Juvenile literature. | Children–Conduct of life–Juvenile literature.
Classification: LCC BF323.L5 J333 2024 (print) | LCC BF323.L5 (ebook) | DDC 153.6/8–dc23/eng/20221213
LC record available at https://lccn.loc.gov/2022051538
LC ebook record available at https://lccn.loc.gov/2022051539

Published in 2024 by
Gareth Stevens Publishing
2544 Clinton Street
Buffalo, NY 14224

Copyright © 2024 Gareth Stevens Publishing

Designer: Claire Wrazin
Editor: Kristen Nelson

Photo credits: Cover Rawpixel.com/Shutterstock.com; p. 5 BearFotos/Shutterstock.com; pp. 7, 9, 19, 21 Monkey Business Images/Shutterstock.com; p. 11 SpeedKingz/Shutterstock.com; p. 13 fizkes/Shutterstock.com; pp. 15, 17 szefei/Shutterstock.com; p. 23 Krackenimages.com/Shutterstock.com; p. 24 (left) studiovin/Shutterstock.com; p. 24 (middle) wee dezign/Shutterstock.com.

Printed in the United States of America

CPSIA compliance information: Batch #CSGS24: For further information contact Gareth Stevens, at 1-800-542-2595.

Find us on

Contents

I listen at school!
It is a rule.

Ms. Shepard is
reading to the class.
Diep and Graham
sit quietly.
They are listening.

The teacher asks
about the book.

Gerald knows
the answer!

He was listening
to the story.

Trini listens
in music class.
She learns the words
to a song.

I listen at home!

Melissa's sister is upset.
She wants to talk.

Melissa is quiet. She nods as she listens.

Frankie's mom calls him
to dinner.
She says to turn off
his show.

Frankie turns it off.

He heard his mom.

He understood.

How can you listen?

Words to Know

book

class

teacher

Index